DATE DUE

WE CAN READ!™

Lou Goes Too!

by Jacqueline Sweeney

photography by G. K. & Vikki Hart
photo illustration by Blind Mice Studio

BENCHMARK BOOKS

MARSHALL CAVENDISH
NEW YORK

This has to be for Matthew, aka Lou

With thanks to Daria Murphy, Reading Specialist,
K-8 English Language Arts Coordinator,
for reading this manuscript with care and for writing
the "We Can Read and Learn" activity guide.

Benchmark Books
Marshall Cavendish Corporation
99 White Plains Road
Tarrytown, New York 10591

Text copyright © 2000 by Jacqueline Sweeney
Photo illustrations copyright © 2000 by G. K. & Vikki Hart
and Mark & Kendra Empey

Library of Congress Cataloging-in-Publication Data
Sweeney, Jacqueline.
Lou goes too! / Jacqueline Sweeney.
p.   cm. — (We can read!)
Summary: Hildy the duck is annoyed to have to take her little brother Lou to the
pond with her, but she realizes how much he means to her when he gets stuck in
the mud and has to be rescued.
ISBN 0-7614-0921-1
[1. Ducks—Fiction. 2. Brothers and sisters—Fiction.]
I. Title II. Series: We can read! (Benchmark Books/Marshall Cavendish)
PZ7.S974255Lo   1999   [E]—dc21   98-43359 CIP   AC

Printed in Italy

3 5 6 4 2

Characters

Mama

Hildy

Lou

Molly

Gus

Ron

Alice

Jim

Tim

Hildy was growing up —
too big to swim with Mama Duck,
too big to swim with Lou.

But Mama had a rule.

"Lou's your little brother.

Lou goes too!"

Hildy waddled to the pond.

Lou went too.

"Go away!" quacked Hildy.

Lou peeped back,
"I go too!"

Hildy hopped up on Pond Rock.

Lou hopped too.

One hop for Hildy.

Two hops for Lou.

Hildy flapped her wings.

SPLASH!

She swam away.

She made up a song:

"Splish—splish, I'm swimming
all around the pond."

She paddled past sleepy Gus—

past Ron the Toad—

past Alice reading to her twins.

Hildy paddled and sang, paddled and sang.

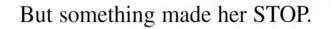

But something made her STOP.

She looked back.

She listened.

17

"Lou?"

quacked Hildy.

"Louis?"

quacked Hildy.

"Louis, where ARE you?"

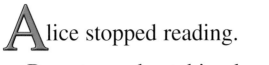

Alice stopped reading.
Ron stopped catching bugs.

Gus was pointing at some weeds.

peep…

sniff…

peep…

sniff…

There was Lou stuck deep in the mud.

23

Ron and Hildy pushed.

Gus and Alice pulled.

"One, Two, HEAVE!

One, Two, HO!

"HEAVE–HO! HEAVE–HO!"

At last Lou was free.

Hildy hugged him

with her soft brown wings.

"I'm sorry I left you," she said.

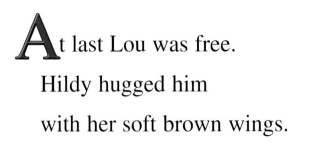

Then Hildy made a rule:

"From this day until
   my brother's big enough
   to reach Pond Rock in just ONE hop—
   Lou goes too!"

WE CAN READ AND LEARN

The following activities are designed to enhance literacy development. *Lou Goes Too!* can help children to build skills in vocabulary, phonics, and creative writing; to explore self-awareness; and to make connections between literature and other subject areas such as science and math.

LOU'S CHALLENGE WORDS

Discuss the meanings of these words and use them in sentences:

brother	bug	flap	peep
point	pond	quack	reach
rule	sniff	song	swim
twin	waddle	weed	wing

FUN WITH PHONICS

Hot Spots on the Pond. Help children strengthen phonics skills by listening for short o words in the story. Give each child small yellow post-its or feathers, if you have them. These represent ducks. Use sheets of blue construction paper for ponds or have children draw ponds of their own. As a parent or teacher reads the story, each child puts a feather or post-it on the pond when a short o word is heard. The child who has the most ducks on the pond at the end of the story wins.

Short o words:

pond	stop/stopped	soft	on
song	hop/hopped	Ron	rock

Poetry Is Just Ducky! Discuss what it means to think something is "just ducky." Children can write a poem about something that makes them feel just ducky. Use rhyming words or short o words from the story to get started.

Rhyming words:

Lou • too • you
peep • deep
hop • stop
on • Ron

30

CREATIVE WRITING

Hildy's Rule. In this story, Hildy made a rule. Discuss what rules are and why it is important to have rules at home and at school. Ask children to think about rules they might want to make if they could write the rules. Then have them write school rules, bus rules, duck rules. ...Let their imaginations rule!

Take Action! In this story, Hildy and her friends had to take action to help Lou. Children can write about a time when they had to help someone who was stuck like Lou or was just in need of a friend. Using action words from the story, parents or teachers can help children understand what an action word is by acting them out. Stories can then be written and shared using many high energy words.

Action words:

looked	listened	stopped	waddled
hopped	flapped	paddled	pushed
pulled	hugged	pointed	quacked
catching	reading	sang	

DUCKY FACTS ABOUT MALLARDS

Help children research ducks. How do ducks float? Why are their feet webbed? Children can record their findings on feather shapes made from white or yellow paper. Feathers may be cut out by following a simple pattern. They can then be attached to the back of a headband for a duck tail of facts. To make the headband, cut strips of yellow, white, or brown paper in three- to four-inch strips. Measure around the students' heads and then staple or glue strips together.

POND LIFE MURAL

Hildy and Lou met several animal friends at Willow Pond. Gus the turtle, Ron the toad, and Alice and her rabbit twins all helped Hildy and Lou. Help children discover the energy and excitement in a pond. Children can research plant and animal life and create a mural depicting pond life. Use paints, crayons, paper, magazine pictures, and odds and ends to create a mural that Hildy, Lou, and their friends would love to visit!

About the author

Jacqueline Sweeney has published children's poems and stories in many anthologies and magazines. An author for Writers in the Schools and for Alternative Literary Programs in Schools, she has written numerous professional books on creative methods for teaching writing. She lives in Stone Ridge, New York.

About the photo illustrations

The photo illustrations are the collaborative effort of photographers G. K. and Vikki Hart and Blind Mice Studio. Following Mark Empey's sketched story board, G. K. and Vikki Hart photograph each animal and element individually. The images are then scanned and manipulated, pixel by pixel, by Mark and Kendra Empey at Blind Mice Studio.

Each charming illustration may contain from 15 to 30 individual photographs.

All the animals that appear in this book were handled with love. The ladybugs and butterflies were set free in the garden, while the others have been returned to or adopted by loving homes.